# Swingers To Captive Lovers - A Wife Watching Multiple Partner Wife Sharing Romance Novel

### Karly Violet

Published by Karly Violet, 2024.

# Swingers To Captive Lovers

# A Wife Watching Multiple Partner Wife Sharing Romance Novel

All Right Reserved © Karly Violet 2024

All rights reserved. No part of this publication may be reproduced, distributed, or transmitted in any form or by any means without the prior written permission of the author, except in the case of brief quotations embodied in critical reviews and certain noncommercial uses permitted by copyright law.

Individuals on the cover are models and are used for illustrative purposes only.

Author's note: All character in this story are 18 years of age and older. This is a work of fiction, any resemblance to real live name or events are purely coincidental.

Be aware: This story is written for, and should only be enjoyed by, ADULTS. It includes explicit descriptions of intense sexual activity between consenting adults.

**Note that this work of fiction resembles a fantasy world, all events taking place are a result of a role play amongst all parties and all parties are fully consenting adults.**

# Chapter One: The Dangers of Banking

"SNE Bank is the premiere banking experience in Denver," Carl Benton, Vice President of Customer Affairs says to us from across his desk. "We are known for catering to those who have a taste for the finer things in life and wish to know that their money is completely secure and guaranteed against loss while here."

"That's the purpose of any bank, though, right?" Raina elbows me after I make the observation and I nearly laugh. However, it bothers me a little to listen to such a scripted statement whenever we look to move our money from one place to another.

"Well, yes. All banks insure the funds deposited within them up to a certain amount."

"But, you will insure all of our money against loss?"

"Of course."

"For a fee, no doubt."

Mr. Benton looks nervously from me to my wife as he replies, "It is a nominal fee, but of course. Your money will be completely safe here and we will give you a half percentage point more interest on the account than what we offer our standard account holders."

I sit forward in my seat. "Oh. So, we would get 2.5% instead of the 2%?"

"Jake, do you have to grill the poor guy so much? He just told us that."

The bank VP nods his head. "That is correct, sir. It's a very good deal when you consider that the other banks in the city do not differentiate between their standard accounts and their executive accounts."

"Wow. Okay." I chuckle as I look over at Raina. "What do you think?"

She shrugs her shoulders. "It sounds okay to me if you're ready to make the transfer."

I look into my wife's brilliant blue eyes and wonder for the millionth time just how it was possible that I came to know her in the first place. We were not running with the same groups of people while in college, but somehow I met Raina and immediately fell in love with her. She's a beautiful woman, but she is also a highly intelligent and independently minded woman. These traits altogether led me to believe she was the one for me from the very beginning. The feeling was not mutual at first, so I had to work on her a little to make her mine. But in due time, we were engaged and then married. For eight years now, we have worked hard to build up our financial portfolio, and now it's time to find a bank that fits the profile of someone with our liquid assets. SNE Bank seems to be the one.

"So, what do you say? Are you all in for our bank?" Mr. Benton smiles widely as he looks at the two of us.

Before either of us can answer, we hear shouting across the bank. I turn to see five men, all dressed in business suits and black masks, walking quickly toward the tellers with bags and guns in their hands.

"Get on the fucking floor! NOW!!!" I pull at my wife's arm as I go to the floor and we both do as instructed by the armed men. "You too, fucker!" the man says as he approaches Mr. Benton. Though stunned at first and not moving, he quickly does as the robber demands.

"No one move! If we see you reach for anything like a phone, you will be shot!" The man doing the talking walks around the bank with a sawed-off shotgun in his hands. "Do not look around. Do as you are told and you will be just fine. Don't fuck with us and we will not fuck with you."

Other robbers in the group are now behind the teller windows collecting whatever money they have in their drawers. The bank vault, open during business hours, has two of the robbers inside taking whatever they can find there. Right now I think about the money that Raina and I are considering moving to this bank. Is this robbery the sort of thing we will need to be concerned about? Mr. Benton told us the bank insures the money here for a small fee, but is that completely true? I don't want to lose three million dollars to a bunch of people with black ski masks over their heads.

"Hurry up, boys," the man in charge says as he watches the crowd. "Get that loot and get out here! We have a plane to catch."

"On the way, boss," the one behind the counter says before jumping over with a bag full of money. He hands it to the one in charge before he goes from person to person to check them for whether they are doing anything they are not supposed to be doing.

Soon, all five robbers are back in the lobby while toting three large bags of cash. The leader goes over to a couple on the floor and tells them to get up. They do and he puts them against the teller counter. He then goes to another couple and does the same thing. My heart begins to race as he approaches us. Raina shakes her head as she looks at him, but her silent plea doesn't matter as he forces us both to our feet. He then looks at the bank VP and gives him instructions.

"Do not call the police and do not activate an alarm for fifteen minutes. Do you understand?"

"Yes, sir," Mr. Benton replies while on the floor.

"These six are coming with us. If we even sniff a cop behind us, they're all dead. Do you understand this?"

"Yes, sir," the VP says to him once again. "Please don't harm them. They are innocent people."

The leader of the robbers drops the barrel of his shotgun down to where it is pointing directly at Mr. Benton's head. "I don't recall asking about your concerns, mister. You will do as you are told or they are dead. Got it?"

"Yes. Of course." Mr. Benton's eyes turn toward us for a moment as the robbers gather us together and bind our hands with zip ties. They then cover our mouths with tape and put a long bandana over our eyes. We are paraded out in a line while holding onto each other's shoulders. I fear for my wife as we are taken outside and told to step up into a van. This could be it. We could be heading to our doom as the robbers close the doors and then start the vehicle. Soon, all of us are on our way somewhere.

"How much?" The leader asks one of them.

"It looks like around twenty g's from the windows and maybe another hundred from the vault."

Another of the robbers complains, "They don't stack so many bills in there like they used to, boss."

"No, they don't. It doesn't matter, though. It's enough to keep us happy until the next one." Though I can't see the man, I get the feeling he is now looking at the six of us they have kidnapped as he says, "You lucky people are going to be spending some time together in the mountains for a couple of days. If you're good, you'll end up going home in one piece. But, if you're assholes, you'll never see the outside world again." He pauses before adding, "We're really not bad people, but we take care of ourselves. Don't fuck with us and we won't fuck with you. It's a straight up promise to you."

"Or, we could just fuck the women for fun," another jokes. I can hear a hand make contact with a face. "Damn, boss, I was just funnin'."

"We're not touching them, boys. They are the reason we have a job, right? We don't want the customers to be unhappy and then pull their money from their banks. I mean, that's just not good customer service."

The men in the van laugh at the odd statement from their leader. I reach over to the person I believe is my wife and soon I can feel her hand and ring. Without a doubt, Raina is right beside me in the van. We hang to each other as we quietly sit throughout the trip to the mountains we have been promised. There are bears and other things in the Rockies that could easily kill and eat all of us, so I hope that they will at least put us in a cabin or house that is well built. A tent would be an invitation to trouble in some parts of the woods.

"Turn here, man," the one known as their boss tells the driver. I can hear the engine slow and then I can feel the turn before the engine picks up speed again. I get the feeling we have just entered an interstate, though I don't know which one. Hopefully we won't be too far into the mountains and the police will be able to find us soon. Whatever happens,

I will do anything to keep my dear wife safe from harm. If I must, I will even lose my life for her.

# Chapter Two: No Way Out

"Come along," someone says to us as they pull at our arms. We are all still blindfolded and tied with zip ties. As we are taken inside somewhere, one of the robbers searches us for our phones and other things. Some of the others protest a little, but they become quiet once they are threatened with getting the butt of a gun against their face. It takes only a couple of minutes for all of us to be seated and the blindfolds are then removed.

"So, this is your home for the next few days," the leader of the bankrobbers says to us as his eyes peer through the holes of his mask at us. "You are in the mountains and there is no one within several miles of this place. As a matter of fact, you have more of a chance seeing a bear or mountain lion than you do of seeing a person out here." He looks around the upper scale cabin where we are sitting. "This is a nice place to spend a little time, so don't bother trying to get out of here. The windows have bars and the door will be screwed shut once we have gone. Do you all understand me?"

Another one of his crew comes around and pulls the tape from our mouths, causing some of us to wince in pain as he does. Gritting my teeth, I look up at the leader and say, "Why not just let us go? You have what you want, right? We won't be able to get to any town before you're fifty miles away, anyway."

The man looks down at me and chuckles. "You don't seem to understand the arrangement here, mister. There are two ways this can go. Either we leave you all here for a couple of days for insurance so that we won't be followed, or we take you out into the fucking woods and blow your heads off. What do you think? Which one sounds better?"

One of the other captives shakes her head and says to him, "Please. My husband and I have young children at home. Let us go."

"Is there someone with them?" the masked man asks.

"Yes. Their grandmother."

"Then, granny had better be ready to watch them a little longer, huh?" He cocks the shotgun he is holding, causing her to cry out as she worries he might shoot her.

"Look, we understand," Raina says to the man. "We won't be any trouble."

He turns to look at my wife. "So, this is the smart one in the group. At least there's one of you to keep the others from fucking up and seeing what happens." The man turns to his comrades and tells them, "Make sure everything is secure before we go."

"Yes, boss," a couple of them say before going to do as he has asked.

"Why are you doing this?" another one of the captives asks him. "You don't have to be so mean, man. This sort of crime is made worse by the fact you have kidnapped six people. Chances are, you could have gotten away by simply having a backup car and a change of clothes."

"Well, look at this guy with the criminal mind," the leader says with a laugh as he walks over to where he's sitting. "I'll bet you've seen the inside of a prison cell, haven't you?"

The man sitting nearby slowly nods his head. "Petty theft."

"Oh. Petty theft. Heaven forbid a guy should be put in jail for petty theft." The other robbers in the room laugh as the masked leader bends down and looks into the other man's eyes. "I've never been to prison but I've scored several banks over the last couple of years. It's a fine science to do that, and I'm doing what I know works. You, on the other hand, got caught with your hand in the cookie jar. Why in fuck's sake would a successful bankrobber take the advice of a guy who gets busted for petty theft? Huh?" Again, there is laughter in the room among the masked men.

For several minutes, we sit in silence as our captors complete their check of the large cabin. One of them approaches the leader and says something before he nods toward those of us who are tied up. Two of the robbers walk over and pull out knives to cut our bindings. It is at this point that the leader decides to give us our final instructions.

"Don't leave the cabin," he says firmly. "Even if you do manage to get something loosened around a window or a door, there will be booby traps waiting for you. We will make sure the outside is locked down so that you can't get out easily, but it would be a shame when the police arrive in a couple of days for them to find pieces of one of you all over the place."

"Two days, then?" one of the women asks.

"Two or three," he replies. "Just keep in mind, if you leave this place before the authorities arrive, you will die. There will be no going back after that. Do you all understand me?"

We all nod or reply that we understand, but I decide to go a bit further with him. "What if there is a health issue with one of us? What then?"

"Don't die," he says flatly. "That's all I can tell you, buddy." He nods at the others and they all slowly back out of the room onto the front porch. After the door is closed, we can hear drilling and other sounds that indicate they are sealing the door behind them. I frown as I look at everyone in the room and realize how worried we all must be for what will happen between now and when the robbers decide to let the authorities know where we are.

"Fuck, man." One of the other men in the group puts both hands on his head as he paces the floor. "Those assholes have locked us in and there's nowhere we can go. I can't even call my parents to let them know we're okay."

"They're okay, Mike," the woman who came with him says. "Don't worry about them right now. We need to make sure there's plenty of water and food here."

"They said there would be," another woman in the group says.

"Yeah, well they don't strike me as all that trustworthy," the first woman replies.

We all begin to make our way through the house to look for anything that could be useful to us. Someone discovers more than enough food in the kitchen while others find pillows and blankets along with three large beds upstairs. The cabin, though located in the middle of the woods, is quite luxurious and must be worth a million dollars or more. Why the bank robbers would put us up in such a place baffles me, but I suppose they have their reasons for doing so.

"The bathrooms work," one of the other men says to us. "And the showers."

"The electricity, too," Raina adds. "It's as if they want us to actually be comfortable while we are here."

One of the men laughs. "Well, they are probably trying to do as little as possible to get a serious kidnapping charge thrown onto them when they get caught."

"If they get caught," the woman with him says.

"No, they'll get caught. Guys like that have it coming to them." He looks at the rest of us and says, "I'm Dominique and this is my wife, Rebecca."

"Hello," she says with a smile and a short wave.

"I'm Raina and this is my husband, Jake," my wife replies.

"Michael and Dara," the other man says while frowning. "Now that we're all fucking acquainted, we should try to get out of this place."

"We can't do that," I warn him. "You heard what that guy told us, right? If we try to get out, there are booby traps waiting for us. I don't know about you, but I would prefer to chill out and just wait for the good guys with guns to show up and rescue us."

Michael laughs. "The cops? Good guys with guns? Fuck them, man. We need to get out of here so that they can't come back and do us in."

"Baby, they're not going to do that," his wife says to him. "You have to calm down."

"I am calm," he growls. "I'm so fucking calm that I just might fall asleep." His dark eyes look around the room as he runs a hand through his thick brown hair. "There's got to be a way out of this place. If we just all look, I'm sure we'll find it."

Michael goes to the other side of the room and checks the bars on the windows. It's apparent that he wants out badly and he would do anything to get out. I'm concerned that he could be experiencing some kind of cabin fever that could become dangerous to the rest of us.

"Is he always like this?" I ask Dara.

She shakes her head. "Mike's a good guy. He really is. It's just that he spent three years in prison for something he did when he was seventeen and since then he doesn't like to be locked up. I'll get him to calm down, though." His wife goes to him and speaks to the agitated man as Dominique comes over to where I'm standing.

"He's gonna pop," he says to me. "That guy is way too tightly strung to be in here with us." Pausing and taking a breath, he soon asks, "What are your thoughts on tying him up?"

I turn to look at the man. "Well, um, I don't like it."

His eyes turn to meet mine. "We might not have a choice if that man goes nuts in here, Jake. Look at him. We've been in here for twenty minutes and he's a total nutcase."

"He's fine. Look, his wife is doing a lot to get him to calm down right now. This is just a fucked up situation and we all have our own ways of dealing with it."

"You and I are calm, man. That dude is nuts." Dominique shakes his head before going back to his wife.

"I don't like this, Jake," Raina says as she puts her arm around my back. "Dominique might be right about him. We might have to tie him up so that he doesn't hurt himself or someone else."

"Why?" I ask while looking over at her. "What has he done so far that would merit that treatment? The guy is just stressed out by the situation. He's not attacking anyone or even making threats."

"No, but he's obviously not happy here."

"Are you?" I ask sarcastically.

"Of course not, but look at him." I turn my eyes to look at Michael once again as instructed by my wife. "He's crying."

"Crying isn't a sign of homicidal mania, honey. We're not tying that guy up, and that's final."

There is some part of me that feels terrible for Michael and his wife. The way he is behaving seems reminiscent of some kind of early trauma that likely filled his life. Prison was a terrible experience for him, but there was probably something else before that which has caused his reaction to this confinement. He seems like a good man overall, and I believe in giving people the benefit of the doubt before passing judgment on them. It's the right thing to do, after all.

"So, what do we do now?" Rebecca asks.

"It will be dark soon," Raina replies. "Maybe we should make a little dinner for the six of us and then just talk?"

"That would be nice," Dara says from behind us as she leads her husband back to where we are standing. Though he doesn't make eye contact with us, he seems to be much calmer now.

"Sure, it would. Maybe we could pass the time along with talking and playing a few games. There must be some games or cards around this place somewhere. It's fully stocked, after all."

"Games?" Dominique raises an eyebrow and chuckles. "Like for kids?"

"Games," her husband tells him. "And you're going to play, sweetheart. Or, you can always sleep by yourself."

The threat causes Dominique to blush a little as he looks at his wife. The embarrassment of such a threat might be good for the man who has already suggested we should tie up one of the other hostages. Maybe for now he will attempt to be more understanding of everyone in the house.

We all go into the kitchen and look at our food options. Raina and Dara begin to work on some of the vegetables while I help Michael prepare some meat that we have pulled out of the freezer. It is our intention that everyone in this cabin will eat well tonight, no matter what situation we currently find ourselves in.

# Chapter Three: Differing Backgrounds

During dinner, we all get to talking about ourselves and what we do for a living. It seems to make sense to get to know the people in the group in order to have some understanding of each other.

"So, what do you do for a living?" Dominique asks me after taking a drink of his water. "You seem like a psychologist when you speak."

I smile. "Actually, the psychologist in the family is my wife." Nodding toward her, I wink. "However, I think some of what she has talked about at home has rubbed off on me. My actual full time thing right now is the stock market."

"You're a trader?" Dara asks.

"I am now, but that wasn't always the case. I started out in real estate and just sort of transitioned into it. Every so often I handle a few accounts for a few people I know and it seems so far I have a golden touch for it."

"And you're filthy rich now, right?" Dominique observes.

"We are very comfortable," I admit. "Thankfully, we didn't have any money in the bank today, though."

"They will cover it," Raina observes. "They will make sure their customers are out of nothing."

"As long as it's not too much and they bought that extra insurance," I remind her. "You know how that manager tried to weasel us into the deal with that information."

"At least you have money," Michael says as he sits back in his chair. "The wife and I own a florist shop and it's going belly-up soon."

"Don't say that, Mike," Dara says to him. "You know I don't like it when you talk like that." She frowns while looking at the rest of us. "I'm sorry about him. He's just a little tense right now."

"Loosen up, man," Dominique says with a smile. "We're all friends here now, right? Those guys in the masks have done that to us."

Michael shrugs his shoulders. "There's nothing to loosen up about. The business is shit and we don't have very many customers. We're going to sink."

His wife shakes her head as she looks sad and angry at the same time. I can only imagine the pain they must feel as they see their flower shop die. It's not an easy thing at all for a business to fail, but it happens more than not. So many people go into business for themselves with the attitude that if they work hard enough it will all work out. That's not always the case.

"Well, I guess it's our turn," Dominique says while looking over at his wife, Rebecca. "I am an insurance adjuster and my wife is a home health consultant. We're from southern California and here to see some friends and family."

"Ah, sunny California," Raina says with a smile. "I love visiting there."

"It really is very nice," Rebecca replies. "The taxes and regulations are terrible, but it's great to be able to go to the beach when you want to."

"I prefer Colorado," I chime in. "The winters here can be really pretty."

"And long," Mike says while shaking his head and smiling. It's good to see his face a little brighter after the sadness following his declaration concerning their failing flower shop.

"Sometimes it stretches on for a bit," I agree. "But there are a lot of nice people here."

"Just not at the bank," Rebecca complains. "I don't understand why guys like that do such a thing to us. All we were doing was minding our own business and getting money for our nephew's birthday. It wasn't as if we were causing them any problems."

"They are walking problems," I tell her. "Guys like that want to be in control and that's probably why they came in there in the first place. The money is good, but that leader of the group seemed more addicted to the power he wielded."

"Fucker," Mike mutters while shaking his head. "If he hasn't been to prison yet, he will eventually. Then I want to see how his punk ass does things."

"Baby, don't talk about that," Dara pleads with him. "We are here now with these wonderful people and we are all in the same boat. It's better if we just keep our minds on what we can do to kill the time."

Dominique gets up from his seat and points a finger toward the living room. "I say we go to that damned door and see if it will budge."

"I don't think that's a good idea," I tell him. "They warned of booby traps."

"Booby traps? They're full of shit," he replies. "Those guys probably wouldn't know how to make a booby trap."

"Yeah, and they might have done it, though," Mike agrees with me. "If we start pushing around on that door, it could set something off. If the house caught on fire, we would be toast; literally."

"If you guys don't have the stomach for it, I do." Dominique leaves the dining room and heads toward the front door. We all get up and follow him, some in our group pleading for him to give up his plan to force the door open. It seems he isn't going to be swayed by any of us, so we get back and watch him kick at the door over and over again.

"Dude, you'll break your foot on that thing," Mike says to him. "They screwed it down with a sheet of plywood. There are probably fifty screws in that thing."

"I don't care!" Dominique continues kicking for several minutes as we watch. After a while, though, he begins to tire and soon he backs away and stares at the door.

"Are you finished, Dom?" his wife asks while placing her hand on her hips.

He catches his breath before looking back at all of us. "Don't you people want out of this shithole?"

"Shithole? At least we're not in the ground," I point out. "Honestly, those guys could have put us in shallow graves up here on the mountain and no one would know. I'm grateful that my wife and I are still upright and walking around."

"Please just come take a seat, okay?" his wife says as she takes his arm. "We need to settle down and rest a little for a while."

The six of us make our way to the living room and I reach for the television remote. Though I hope to find that there is some sort of satellite television service here, I soon discover this is not the case. Whoever uses this cabin has cut off the service for now.

"No entertainment, either," Dominique complains. "Like I said before, it's a shithole."

"We have what we need," Raina says to him. "As for entertainment, it would be fun to get to know each other much better with a question and answer game, don't you think?"

"A question and answer game?" Dara sits forward in her seat. "How is this played?"

"Well, one person starts it off and asks another person something about them or their life. You have to answer truthfully."

"Is that really a game, though?" Rebecca says to Raina. "It sounds like an interview."

"A fun interview," my wife tells her. "Anyway, it will only be enjoyable if everyone participates."

Dominique shakes his head. "This doesn't sound so great, to be honest."

"Just try it," his wife replies.

"Okay, then. Who will be first?" Raina asks the group.

"I will," Dara replies.

"Okay, Dara. You can ask anything of any of the people here besides your husband."

"Anything?" She grins while looking at Raina.

"Anything, yes."

"Alright." Dara looks at the people in the room with her before settling on Rebecca. "How old were you when you got your first kiss?"

Rebecca raises an eyebrow and then thinks for a moment. "Well, let me see, I think I was twelve and it was a guy named Samuel in middle school."

"Was it nice?" Dara asks.

"Just one question at a time, please," I say with a giggle.

"Very nice." Rebecca winks at the other woman as her face turns pink. "Of course, not as nice as my dear Dom's sweet kisses."

Dominique's face turns a little red as he looks away and shakes his head. It's apparent he's very taken by his wife and the compliment got to him. Not quite as tough as he would like to make us all believe, he's actually a softy deep down.

"Okay, me next?" Rebecca asks as she looks at me.

"Sure. We'll go with the person who answered the previous question each time. Just try to choose someone other than Dara for your question."

Rebecca's eyes move across everyone until they settle upon me. She smiles wickedly for a moment before asking, "Who did you give your virginity to and at what age?"

"Oh, shit," I say as I feel my cheeks getting warm.

"You have to answer her," Raina says with a laugh. She knows the answer to this already, which is why she finds it so amusing.

I sigh before I tell her, "Alright, you have to understand, I was really wet behind the ears anyway. I mean, I hadn't even had my first kiss yet."

"Dude," Dominique says as he perks up and looks at me.

"Her name was Irene and she was in my senior English class. Well, one day we decided to go for a walk by a nearby river and while there she asked if I had been given a blowjob before. I told her no, and then she just opened my pants and gave me one."

"That's a hummer, not losing your virginity," Mike points out.

"Well, when she was finished sucking on me, she wanted me to have sex with her. We were both virgins and Irene didn't want to graduate from high school as one. So, we had sex right there along the side of the river."

"Did you have anything to lie on?" Rebecca asks.

"Nope. She bent over a fallen tree and I did my thing."

Raina laughs hard as she puts her hand on my shoulder. "I'm sorry, baby! I can't help it!"

"Dammit, honey," I say while grimacing. She's heard me tell this story at least twice before, but each time she finds it more and more hilarious.

"Damn, man. You had an interesting one, that's for certain," Mike says as he shakes his head. "I lost mine in bed with an older woman."

"An older woman?" I say to him.

"Yeah. She was twenty-two and I was seventeen. If she had been caught with me, my mother would have probably filed charges against her. Still, we had a great time."

"And we got married not long after that," Dara says with an impish grin.

"Nice! Robbed the cradle." Dominique looks over at me. "I guess it's your turn now, right?"

I nod my head. "It seems that way." Looking at Dominique, I ask, "What is the worst thing that's ever happened to you?"

"Do you mean besides this bullshit today?" he asks.

"Of course."

"Well, I guess the worst thing to happen to me was when I got into a fight with my best friend, Kevin Durmante. We were thick as thieves until he decided to tell me that I didn't know shit about my own job. So, I clocked him in the eye and we haven't spoken since then."

"How long ago was that?" I ask.

"Eleven years ago," he replies. "The man didn't like to be nice to anyone, especially to me. I guess he thought it was okay to treat his friend like a pile of shit that day and I wasn't in the mood to take it."

"I've told him that he should call Kevin and apologize, but Dom is very proud and won't do that," his wife tells us.

"There's no reason to apologize to a man like that," he tells her.

Dominique soon looks at Raina and asks, "Do you like anal?"

"That's a rude question," his wife scolds him.

"Wow. That's a question I didn't expect," my wife tells him as I begin to get a little turned on by the sexual nature of it. "Um, sure. As long as it's done right and there's plenty of lube involved."

This answer from Raina seems to turn on the other men in the group as we all become quiet and stare at my wife. The attention she is getting now from Mike and Dominique arouses my cock enough that I begin to get a fairly solid hardon.

"Okay, I think maybe that's enough of that for now," I tell the group. "We really should get some sleep if we can."

"We want the first bedroom upstairs," Dara says to us. "If that's alright with the rest of you."

"I'm good with whatever," Raina replies. The others do not seem to object to this request and soon we are all heading upstairs to the bedrooms there.

Though we have been in the cabin for no more than six hours, I can feel the tension in the air between the six of us. We have gone quite a way in trying to keep that tension from affecting us negatively, but it's there nonetheless. I hope we can keep things civil between us during the duration of our stay here in the cabin. If not, things could become very ugly very quickly.

# Chapter Four: Passing the Time

"We have board games," Rebecca says as she and Dara walk into the living room the next morning with three of them. "The closet in one of the bedrooms is stacked full of them."

Dominique scoffs at his wife. "Those are for children, Rebecca. You know I don't like games for kids."

"What's wrong, Dom, you don't like to play games?" I ask as I look over at him.

He shakes his head. "They are for children, man. When was the last time you played *Sorry?*"

"Maybe when I was twelve or thirteen," I reply.

"My point exactly. It's not like that game is for adults."

"Trivial Pursuit," Dara offers. "It's for teens and adults, right? It might be fun to play for a while."

Mike sighs from the sofa nearby. "Baby, you know that I don't have as much education as some of the others here. It wouldn't really be fair, would it?"

"Are you saying you're stupid?" Dominique asks the other man with a grin.

"I'm smart enough, but maybe I don't have as much time in the books as some of you. It's nothing to be ashamed of."

"No, it's not," I agree. "If there was a question about plants, you might easily beat us on it. For psychiatry, my wife would clean up very well. I think that's the way the game works, though. It goes after all sorts of strengths. Whether you have a college degree or not, I would bet that you could do quite nicely, Michael."

He shakes his head. "I don't feel like doing that."

"Understood," I say as I look at the two women. "Any other ideas?"

"For a childhood game?" Dara giggles. "We could always play spin the bottle like I did when I was a teenager."

My wife laughs with her. "That could sometimes become a really naughty game, Dara. I don't think these guys would want to be a part of that."

"How do you play it?" Dominique asks.

His wife explains, "You put a bottle in between a ring of people and then spin it to decide who will do what."

"How do you decide the *what*, though?"

"Sometimes you can draw a piece of paper with it written down on it or even decide what order the things will be done no matter who ends up doing it. The bottle points toward the person at the end of the spin who will have to do the thing on the paper."

"Sounds stupid," Dominique claims.

"Not with adult rules," his wife tells him.

"Whoa," Raina says. "Are you serious about doing that? It gets very intense if you put adult situations on those little pieces of paper."

"How serious?" Dominique asks, his interest piqued by this revelation.

"Use your imagination," I reply. "Anything can go on the papers."

We all look at each other before Michael asks, "Who decides what gets put on those papers?"

Rebecca answers, "We could each fill out two or three and not tell the others what we put on them. Then, we put them in the pot to be drawn before the bottle is spun."

"There have to be limits, though," I point out. "No sex acts, for example."

Michael smiles. "That's the fun of it, though."

"Not if you end up with a piece of paper that says you will have to suck my dick," I say as I look over at him. "Would you want to do that?"

The other man frowns. "Fuck no."

"Me neither."

"So, anything else goes?" Dominique asks with keen interest. "Anything adult oriented?"

"Within reason," Raina replies. "If the others in the group feel it's just too much, we can veto it. Does that sound fair to everyone?"

There seems to be a general consensus over the premise of the game, so my wife goes to a desk in the living room to find some pieces of paper. After tearing them smaller, she hands them out along with pencils and pens. Dominique finishes off his sparkling water and then hands over the glass bottle to be spun. Everything seems to be coming together as we all become excited over what will soon happen during the game.

"So, first spin goes to Dom and then he will draw a paper," Dara says after we all try to guess a number she wrote on a piece of paper. "Then we will go counterclockwise."

Dominique spins the bottle and it lands on me. I take a breath as he looks cautiously at me and then draws a slip of paper. He reads it out loud for us to hear.

"Stand up and act like a rooster for ten seconds." Dominique looks at those in the circle. "What the fuck is this? What a shitty thing to do."

"Honestly, it was mine," I say while shaking my head.

"He hates doing that sort of thing," Raina laughs. "Jake has screwed himself on this."

I take a breath and shake my head while looking at my wife. Standing to my feet, I move my arms to simulate those of a bird or chicken and then begin to cluck as I step around like one. Those in the circle begin to laugh as I do so, with Michael even suggesting I need to crow to pull off the schtick. So, I crow, and by the time I have finished even Dominique has found some humor in what I have done to myself.

"That was a terrible impression of a cock," Dominique laughs. This leads to more laughter from the group as well.

Dominique and his wife are both very attractive people. He is darker in complexion than the rest of us, perhaps Hispanic, with black hair and dark brown eyes. His typical southern California accent tells me he likely grew up there and that he might know some Spanish, but not much. His wife, on the other hand, is petite and lighter colored, though still with a hint of ethnicity that could be Hispanic or Native American, but I cannot be certain. Her hair is dark brown and her eyes a lighter brown.

She is a shapely woman with a nice ass and D-cup breasts, attractive by any standard.

Next is Rebecca, and she spins the bottle to see who will be next to be given something to do. The bottle, however, seems to have a mind of its own as it stops in her direction.

"That's weird," she chuckles. "But I guess I'm going to tell myself what to do." Rebecca reaches into the pot and pulls out a piece of paper. After unfolding it, her eyes grow wide.

"What is it, Becca?" her husband asks.

She raises her eyebrows before saying to him, "Uh, well..." Rebecca hands the sheet of paper to Dominique and his eyes widen as well.

"What is it?" Raina asks.

"It's something that may or may not be okay with the group," he tells her. "Someone put on here that she needs to show her chest."

"What?" I say with nervous laughter. "Who wrote that?" No one in the group immediately answers the question.

"Is there anyone who votes to toss this one?" Raina asks the group.

"No, wait," Rebecca interrupts. "You know what, I'm not afraid of what that little piece of paper asks me to do." She stands to her feet and then pulls her t-shirt up and over her head to reveal her cream colored bra. The beautiful woman then reaches between the bra cups and unfastens the bra so that she can remove it. We are all in a bit of shock as we get a look at her soft, round breasts with two dark pink nipples sitting on the front of them.

"Damn," Michael says as he stares at her chest. "I can't believe you actually did it."

"It was you, wasn't it?" Dominique says while glaring at the other man. "You're the sicko who asked to see my wife's boobs."

"Hey, in all fairness, I didn't know who would get it. It could have been a dude who showed off his chest."

"Fucking pervert," Rebecca's husband complains.

"Stop it," she says as she puts her bra back on. "It's just a fun game, Dom. No harm done here." Rebecca winks at Michael. "I hope you liked what you saw."

Michael's face turns red as his wife, Dara, says something in his ear. I'm sure it's not the nicest thing she's ever said to him as she doesn't seem too pleased to know that her husband put that down one of his little sheets of paper.

"Next," Raina says as she tries to move things along. Dara looks at the bottle and then spins it, the end of it landing on my wife. She then reaches for a piece of paper and reads it.

"Fuck, what the hell now?" Dara laughs.

"Read it," her husband says to her. "Go ahead."

"Okay. Well, um, Raina needs to stand up and turn around before pulling down her pants and undies to moon me."

"Moon you?"

"Yeah, that's what it says."

Michael laughs hard. "What are the odds that two of my three are drawn that quickly?"

I smile as I see how funny he finds this to be. Not only that, it seems like the perfect thing for my sweet wife to have to do in front of the rest of us. Raina isn't exactly the type to willingly show off her body, anyway.

"Dammit" she mutters while turning around. My wife then pulls down her pants and her panties while covering her pussy. She shakes her ass around in the direction of the woman across from her as we all laugh.

"Nice ass," Dominique comments with a grin. "Very nice."

"You don't have to be so happy about it, husband," Rebecca tells him after smacking his chest with her hand.

For the next several spins, there are a variety of things we are asked to do, from simply making a silly face to showing off our feet or our piercings. No one in the group has anything more than an ear or navel piercing, so it seems that we are safe from seeing any more breasts tonight. As things wind down and we begin to get tired, Raina and I go to the kitchen to talk for a moment.

"Did you see the way Mike was laughing?"

"Yeah, I caught that. He loved that game."

My wife nods in agreement. "We need to keep doing things like this in order to help him adjust to this, Jake. I would hate to see him have a mental break over our situation."

"Yeah, I agree. You know, it's not exactly terrible what has happened to us, though. We are free to move around the house and there are plenty of food, drinks, and other things here for us. Those robbers seemed to have thought of just about everything to make sure we could survive this."

"Or they just picked out someone's vacation home and stuck us inside," she replies.

"Maybe so. Anyway, you're right about him. Mike needs something to keep his mind on so he doesn't see this place as a prison. I get the feeling he didn't have the best time while locked up."

"I spoke to Dara a little today, and she told me that things were very bad for him. He was beaten in prison several times and there's a possibility other things happened as well. She doesn't know for certain because he won't talk about it much with her. No matter what happened, though, he was severely affected by prison life. We need to keep this from being a prison for him or anyone else here."

"Yeah, we do."

My wife, Dr. Raina Williams, is the most beautiful woman in the house right now. She is petite, blonde, and she has the most brilliant blue eyes that will stare right through someone. I love her dearly and she loves me just as much. We have been a great couple together, and this has made us so much stronger when things happen. Though I didn't foresee being put into a house and barricaded inside, I'm glad to have Raina with me. She completes me in every way and makes me stronger than I could ever be on my own.

# Chapter Five: Growing Interest

The next day is even more daring as Dominique suggests after breakfast we enjoy the minibar he has broken into while playing a game of strip poker.

"That would be taking things much further," Rebecca points out to her husband. "Are you sure you want to do that? I suck at poker in the first place."

Her husband takes a drink from a small bottle of whiskey and replies, "Sure. Why not just let it all hang out, right? We can see each other just like everyone saw you last night."

"And my ass," Raina adds to the conversation.

I swallow hard and tell the group, "If we did this, everyone would have to be onboard with it and okay with being naked in front of everyone else. There's no easy way to do strip poker if people refuse."

"And there have to be rules about what constitutes clothing and what does not," Mike points out. "Rings and hair ties wouldn't count."

"Shirts, bras, pants, shorts, and panties," Dominique replies.

"Not shoes?" Dara asks.

"Nah. Why do the shoes and socks when it just takes too damn long?"

"You're a little tipsy already, aren't you?" his wife asks while shaking her head. "That's why you're so into this idea, Dom."

He shrugs. "I've had a couple of these tiny bottles," he answers her. "Not as much as you would think."

"Okay, so who would want to play?" It takes a moment, but everyone ends up raising their hands. I'm surprised at us, but I can see why we would want to do this. There is a distinct sexual energy between those in this cabin, and due to this we are much more receptive to the idea that we can do things that are a little more risque.

I begin as the dealer for the first round, putting seven cards in front of each person. I then discuss the rules so that everyone understands the rules and how the game will go. As we begin to play, there are those who are forced to fold. This allows them to take off an item of clothing of their choice. Toward the end of the hand, Rebecca and I are the last two with hands.

"I call," I say to her as I look over at the woman. "What do you have?"

She lays down her cards. "I think that's a straight."

"It is," I agree as I look at them. I then put my cards down and say to her, "Flush."

"Wait, what does that mean?" Rebecca asks her husband.

"Well, that means you have to take off an item of clothing." Her face turns red, even though she must remove only her shirt or pants. We have already seen her breasts, so doing so shouldn't be much of a problem for her.

Rebecca drops her shirt into the floor behind her and smiles nervously. "Hopefully I learn this game so I can win a hand or two as well."

"You will," her husband assures her.

We continue to play our hands, some winning and others losing, until my wife, already topless and without her pants, stands up to remove her small pair of panties. My cock is hard as she reaches down and grips the waistband of her panties before pushing them to the floor.

"Shit," I hear Michael say as he looks at Raina's soft, waxed pussy.

My wife's face turns red as she sits back down on the floor and crosses her legs. Not once before in our marriage has she shown off so much of herself to anyone but me or her doctor. Though she turns to look at me with some expectation that I will comfort her with some words, I have none to give. Not after enjoying the show along with the others in the room.

"Wow," Dom says as he licks his lips.

"You guys took a little too long to look at her," Dara says to the men. "And you didn't look at Rebecca or me that way."

"She's the first one to take off her panties," Mike says to his wife. "You still have yours."

"Fine." Dara stands up and pulls down her panties in protest. "There it is. Bush and all."

My cock becomes even harder as I look at the woman' blonde pubic hair, carefully pruned to where it is mostly just a landing strip above her very nice clitoris. I'm not so sure I will be able to keep the sight of my growing penis away from the others since all I have left on is my underwear.

"He's hard," Rebecca says about Mike. "Look at that. It's poking out of his shorts."

"Dammit." He struggles to push it back inside while shaking his head.

"You know, it's really unfair that the guys haven't shown us much yet," Raina says about us. "I think you should all stand up and take off the rest of your clothes so we can see something interesting as well."

There is a daring look from my wife that causes me to suddenly stand to my feet. I'm hard as I ever have been as I pull down my briefs and the others look at my hard johnson. Rebecca gasps a little and says something to Dara beside her before they both smile. My face turns red as I watch the other two men do the same thing to show what they have as well.

"They're all hard," Dara giggles.

"Yeah, so?" Dominique replies. "We get that way sometimes. It doesn't always mean that we're horny."

Dara reaches over and touches Dom's cock, causing him to flench. "Sorry, I just had to do that."

Rebecca smiles. "Grab it. He won't stop you."

"Becca," her husband says to his wife. Dara does as she suggests, reaching over again to take hold of Dominique's large cock. His body quivers as she does.

"My turn," I hear Rebecca say as she gets up and comes over to me. She reaches down and takes hold of my manhood as well and Raina says nothing to her. Instead, she also reaches for an available cock, which happens to be Michael's.

"Damn," I say as she begins to rub it. "Fuck."

"You're really hard," my wife says to Michael as she pulls on it. "And you're precoming a little."

I watch as Raina uses the other man's precome as a lubricant so that she can slide her hand over the tip of his hard cock. He flinches a little, but Michael doesn't tell her to stop what she's doing. Instead, he stands there nearly motionless as Raina uses her small, soft hands over the length of his shaft as well as his large balls. He swallows hard after a couple of minutes before suddenly spurting on the floor below.

"Wow!" Raina runs her hands over his cock slowly as she watches him ejaculate. "You didn't tell me you were about to come, Mike!"

He says nothing to her as he bites his lower lip and empties the content of his balls onto the floor. Michael obviously enjoys the feeling of my wife's hands on his cock as she helps him to express every last drop of his semen from his body.

"Oh, hell," I say as I feel my own spunk about to rocket out of me.

Rebecca smiles. "Are you going to come, Jake?"

"Yeah, I am. Fuck. Oh, fuck...*ahhhh...AHHHHH!!!*" I spurt hard, my special sauce landing on Dara's feet nearby as Rebecca pulls hard on me. *"Ohhhhh...FUCK!!! FUCK!!! Mmmmm..."*

"There you go, baby," Rebecca says as she giggles and continues to stroke my throbbing penis. "That's the way it's done." She smiles at her husband and asks, "Why haven't you gotten off, yet, Dom?"

"I don't want to," he lies. "Just leave me alone."

Dara giggles. "You don't think I can get you to come?"

"No," he says to her resolutely, though his face is red from what she's been doing to him.

"I'll bet you will." Dara goes down to her knees and opens her mouth, taking in Dominique's cock slowly. His body shudders as she draws the head of his manhood all the way to the back of her throat and sucks hard on him.

"Dammit. Oh, dammit." He grits his teeth together as he watches the woman on her knees feast on his organ. "No. Fuck. I won't do it."

"You'll do it," his wife giggles. as she smiles at him. "I know you too well, baby. I've seen you come so many times. You like her doing that for you, don't you?"

"Fuck. Fuck." His face tightens into a pained expression as he tries to hold back from losing his wad into Dara's mouth.

"Let go," Rebecca tells him. "Do it for me, baby."

He looks at his wife and then suddenly comes inside the other woman's mouth. *"GAAAAHHHH!!! FUCK!!! OOHHHHHH!!!"* Dominique's cock showers the back of Dara's throat with so much semen that she gags a time or two as she struggles to swallow the full load. Her lips remain tightly sealed around his fleshy pole, though, as Dara collects all of his ball's soup. *"Dammit! FUCK!!!"*

As Dominique finishes off in her mouth, we all take a look at each other. There's something about what has just happened, and it seems almost as if things might go a bit further until I hear Raina say, "We have to think about what this means before we just go head first into it."

"What? I think we all know where this is going," Dare tells her as she wipes Dom's jism from her lips and face.

"Just stop and think before anyone has sex, okay? Are we all sure that's what we want?"

I look at the others in the room. There is a little doubt on some of their faces as they consider what my wife has said. A handjob or even a blowjob is not the same as full intercourse. We would be having a much more intimate form of sex if that were to happen between any of us, and my wife is correct in stating that we must be careful about doing so.

"Yeah, we should take a little time this afternoon and just think," I agree.

"What if there are some of us ready to have sex?" Rebecca asks.

"Honey, what?" Dom shakes his head as he looks sternly at his wife.

"Why don't we just find something else to do that doesn't involve sex, okay?" Michael reaches for his wife's hand. They pick up their things and walk out of the room for now. The rest of us also pick up our clothes and retreat to different parts of the cabin.

I for one feel a little ashamed of letting Rebecca give me that handjob. The blowjob that Dominique received from Dara also seemed to take him by surprise. The six of us barely know each other, yet here we are trying to become more sexually active with each other. There are dangers in this, and I think Raina, as a psychologist, began to see this. She knows more than anybody here the importance of thinking before acting. Though agreeing with her in principal, there is a part of me that was ready to fuck Rebecca. It would have taken very little convincing to do so before I was given the handjob by her.

# Chapter Six: Of Like Minds

"What did you think of what happened in the living room?" Raina asks as we sit in one of the bedrooms alone. I've been thinking about this since we left the living room nearly an hour ago.

"I don't know, honey. The tension in there was huge and I'm afraid someone was about to do something if you hadn't stopped it."

She nods her head. "Did you want her?"

"Who?"

"Rebecca. Did you want to have sex with her while she was doing that to you?" Raina's blue eyes look intently at me as she waits for my response.

"Raina, that's not fair. We were both involved in what happened in there."

"That's a yes, then?" I can feel my wife's stare as she waits for clarification from me.

"What the hell can I say?" I ask. "You're going to judge me no matter what I say or do, Raina. I'm screwed in this."

She smiles at me. "No, you really aren't my love." Raina looks at me as if I'm crazy. My wife is probably thinking that I'm just as horny as any of the other guys in that living room. Honestly, she's probably right. I am a horny guy, and I really would like to have sex with Rebecca.

"Look what was happening in there was at the spur of the moment. It really wasn't the sort of thing that most people would be involved in, right?" I can see that my wife is really not buying the argument.

"But you really wanted her, Jake. I could see it in your face. You were hard and you wanted her so badly."

"Honey, I was hard because she had her hand on my cock."

My wife and I sit quietly and just look at each other. I suppose we are both wondering just how far we would have actually gone had things continued. Maybe I would have allowed a little more than I should have, but I think my wife probably would have as well. We are both human, after all. We like the same sort of things, including sex. Raina and I have often laid in bed and wondered what it would be like to have other people in bed with us. We've never acted on this, but it's something we have talked about a little bit in our fantasies.

"So what about it? Jack, do you want to have sex with Rebecca?" Her steely blue eyes look at me as she awaits an answer.

"I think I do. But you know me, Raina, I would never do anything that you would not allow me to do. I'm not the sort of husband who does that to his wife."

"Are you saying that if I tell you it's okay, you would actually do that with her?" My wife's eyes look at me and I looked back at her. We both know the answer to this, but I guess we're afraid to really say what it is.

"You saw what happened in there, Raina. Everyone was into what was going on. They all want to do more with each other. What if we did more than what we were doing earlier? What if we give in to what we're feeling and experiencing? Would that really be so bad?"

I know that what I'm proposing to my wife sounds crazy to her. For nearly ten years we've been married to each other, and we've always been faithful to her. Not once have I thought of even having an affair with another woman, and I'm sure she could say the same thing. My wife and I have been fully devoted to each other, and I have no doubt that we would continue to be devoted to each other no matter what happens between us and the other people in this cabin. We are human, after all. We have needs, wants and desires that could be fulfilled here.

"I'm not sure I know what to say, Jake. What you are asking me to allow you to do is to have sex with another woman. We've never even talked about this very seriously."

"But we have talked about it, honey. We've had sex while talking about our fantasies. You and I have talked so much about it that for a time I thought we were actually going to do it. Of course we didn't, but that's just the way things go sometimes."

"Does that mean you would allow me to have sex with one of the men, Jake?"

"Yes it does."

Raina shakes her head as she considers what I'm saying. Though she might be concerned about the consequences of such actions, she knows that we both want this. We both want to know what it's like to be sexually active with another person. To be intimate with them.

"Do you think the others are talking about this right now?" she asks.

"More than likely, yeah." I reply.

"If something does happen between us and some of the other people here, will it affect our marriage?" Raina seems truly concerned as she asks me this question. She is a psychologist, after all.

She's probably sitting there and analyzing me as we speak. It's the sort of thing she often does when we're talking together and she's trying to figure out whether I'm telling the truth, lying, or bending the truth a little to fit my argument. I have to admit that sometimes I do bend the truth a little. But I rarely lie to my wife about such important things.

"What would you want to do with Rebecca?" she asks.

"What do you think? Look, I'll tell you the truth; I really feel very attracted to her. Rebecca is an incredibly beautiful woman. I'm sure you can see why I would want to do a few things with her in bed."

"What exactly would you do, Jake? Just tell me." My wife crosses her arms as she glares at me. "Would you want her to give you a blowjob? Or maybe you would like her to spread her legs for you?"

"Oh, come on, Raina. Do you really need to play by play of what I would like to do with another woman?" I shake my head and laugh as I look back at my wife.

"Maybe I do. Maybe I want to know what it is my husband wants to do with another woman?"

"Okay then," I say as I chuckle. "I'd like to lay her on the bed and put her legs back and fuck the hell out of her. For you, dear?"

I know what I've said to her sounds a little harsh. Unfortunately, I feel like my wife needs to hear it in this tone. We both feel the same thing as it concerns all of us in the cabin together. There is a tension here, an energy that we both feel. We both know it's here. Though Raina isn't quick to let on, she feels it as well. I know that she does. I saw her with Michael and I saw how badly she wanted him. Given the opportunity, I think she would probably let him spread her legs too.

My wife walks over to the bed where I'm sitting and she has a seat beside me. Putting her hand on my knee, she tells me, "Jake, I understand what you're feeling right now. It's true that I'm feeling some things as well, and I also have some urges that are beginning to show up. But if we do this, it's going to be completely different for us for the rest of our marriage. We will always know that we've had sex with other people during our marriage. It does worry me a little that it could change how we act towards each other."

Reaching my hand over to her face, I say to her, "Honey, you don't have to worry about that. I promise you I will never leave you. I will always love you as my one and only wife, and there is no one else for me. No one here in this cabin will ever replace you, and I can never love anyone any more that I love you."

We began to kiss passionately. My hands move all over her body and Raina's hands move all over mine. We pull close together and I can feel the heat from her body. My wife and I have always had an active sex life. Our lovemaking has been wonderful over the years, and I can't imagine doing anything that would take that away from us. I love her so much and I yearn for her so much that I sometimes cannot stand being without Raina for very long. This is one of those times as I pull her to me and slip my hand under her shirt to find her breast.

"Fuck, baby," she says as I find her hardening nipple and pull at it. "Damn, you're turning me on."

We kiss hard as our clothes come off and our hands move over our naked bodies. My hand finds her wet spot and soon I am fingering my love. Raina grinds her pussy into my hand as I find her G-spot and her back arches, a powerful orgasm overtaking her. She rides the wave of her climax before coming back down and pleading with me to enter her with my hard manhood. I quickly do as she asks, and soon her legs are over my shoulders as my balls collide with her perky asshole.

"Holy shit," I moan as I get deep inside Raina's tight pussy. "Oh, fuck, you're so hot, baby. You're so fucking hot."

Our two bodies continue working against each other on top of the bed until finally I feel my balls ache and my shaft become tense. I release my manly broth into the dark, wet confines of Raina's sweet honeypot, filling her until some of my cream and her pussy juices come out from around my cock. The bed is a mess as we finish having sex, and we are soon in each other's arms while basking in the glow of our dual orgasms.

"All that because you are horny for another woman?" my wife asks with surprise.

"I think so, yeah," I answer with a laugh. "That doesn't make much sense, does it?"

She smiles. "You know, I think it does. Masters & Johnson researched just this topic at one time, Jake. Maybe they were onto something."

"Those were the sex doctors, right?"

"Researchers. Yes."

"Well, I'm beginning to like them, then," I say with a grin on my face.

We soon get up and get dressed after we have enjoyed each other's company a while longer. Raina takes my hand and holds it to her chest.

"This is my heart, Jake. Don't forget that it beats for you, okay? No matter what happens in this house, it will always beat only for you."

I lift her hand to my chest as well. "The same goes for me, honey. I'm not seeking another wife. All I want is to see where things go while we are here. I think it might be really exciting for us. Don't you?"

She nods her head. "You know, I think it just might be. Just don't forget me in all the crazy stuff that could happen, though. I'm your wife. Not Rebecca or Dara."

"You know I will be your hubby forever, baby." I kiss her once more before we leave the bedroom. We are getting hungry and there is plenty in the kitchen we can cook up for a meal. Besides, I'm anxious to see where the others stand when it comes to what Raina and I have just talked about.

# Chapter Seven: Giving in to Temptation

We all sit down at the dinner table to talk about what happened between us earlier in the day. Raina and I have come to agree that things can progress, but that depends on the feelings of the others in the group.

"Are we talking about sex?" Dara asks as she looks at my wife.

"Possibly. It would really be up to each person what they are comfortable with, though. If you don't want to participate, you don't have to."

"Holy shit," Mike chuckles. "Sex with strangers."

"We're not exactly strangers anymore," I point out. "We've all been a little sexually involved already."

"But, there hasn't been any real intercourse, has there?" Dominique makes his remark as Rebecca is noticeably silent. "That's a step in a different direction altogether."

"That's true," I say while nodding my head. "No one here is suggesting that this would be just a quickie sort of thing and then we can all part ways. It will probably be at least another day before the robbers tell the authorities where we are."

A silence fills the room as we all think about what is being said. Most of us appear to be somewhat agreeable that some form of sexual stuff can happen between us, but others such as Dominique seem not so certain of this. I can understand what his reservation is as I look at his beautiful wife beside him.

"What if we split up into different couples?" Raina suggests.

"Do you mean we all swap spouses?" Dara asks.

"That's exactly what I mean. We could all then get to know the other person and see if there's anything there we want to pursue."

Mike smiles. "That would be interesting, wouldn't it?"

"And who would you propose I go with?" Dom asks.

"Me, of course," my wife says to him confidently. Her strong response seems to have an effect on the other man.

"I want to talk to Rebecca," Mike says as he smiles at her. Rebecca returns a very brief, sweet smile.

"This is crazy," Dominique complains. "What will this serve to do?"

"It will only allow us to get to know another person. That's all." Raina grins at Dom and asks, "Are you brave enough to spend some time with me, Dominique?"

His face pinkens a little as he looks at the rest of us. I'm not sure what he's thinking right now, but I'm sure it probably has something to do with the way my wife continues to challenge him. If he backs down and tells her to pound sand, that would undermine him in other ways. It might tell his own wife that he's afraid of what could happen if they split up.

"Come on, man. Let's do this. I'll be nice to your wifey."

"Fuck you," Dominique answers Mike. He then looks at me. "Rebecca should go with you, Dara with me, and then Raina with the asshole."

"No problem. She's sexy," Mike replies with a smile.

"Is that okay with the rest of you?" Raina asks. Everyone seemed agreeable, so we each take our new partner to a different part of the living room to talk. Rebecca seems excited as she goes with me to a sofa near one of the windows.

"Hello again," she says to me as we sit down.

"Hi, Rebecca," I reply.

"Call me Becca."

"Alright, Becca. So, where do we begin?"

She shrugs. "What is your favorite sex position."

I blush. "I think we are supposed to take things a little slower. Shouldn't we talk about other things before getting to the sex stuff?"

She focuses her brown eyes on me as she uses her fingers to move her hair around her ear. "Well, okay. I guess I can tell you something about me and then you can tell me something about you."

"Let's do that," I say with a smile.

"Alright. Let's see. Well, um, I was born in Arizona and I've never met my father."

"Oh? I'm sorry about that."

"It's okay. If a person doesn't ever have something, can they really miss it?" Rebecca's face shines as she smiles at me. "Also, I went to college and was a stripper for a couple of years to help pay the bills."

"What?"

"A stripper." She turns her eyes to look down at her hands briefly before focusing them on me once again. "Does that disappoint you?"

"No, not at all," I assure her. "It does explain why you didn't mind taking off your top during spin the bottle, though."

"I've learned to be very open with who I am." She looks back at her husband, who is talking to Dara at the moment. "Dom is a little more reserved than I am, and that sometimes worries him. I think he's afraid I might get bored with him and go find a new lover."

"That's not good."

"No, it's not. Sometimes it affects my friendship with other men. I wish he would just loosen up a little and enjoy life more."

I sigh as I look at Dominique with my wife. They seem to be enjoying talking to each other immensely. Raina has the uncanny ability to really connect with other people, which is probably why she makes such a great psychologist. Without her, there would be a lot of people who would lead a much sadder life. She's a wonderful woman and a great therapist when it comes to those she really cares for.

"What do you expect out of this, Becca?"

She raises an eyebrow. "What do you mean?"

"I mean, what do you want to happen between us as we talk? Do you want to have something more physical with me?"

"I think I proved to you earlier just how much I like you, baby." She smiles as she looks at my crotch. My cock swells as if Rebecca's gaze controls it completely.

"You did," I admit.

"You want me, don't you?" she asks.

Swallowing hard first, I tell her, "I do, but I'm worried what that could mean for me and my wife. She's worried that I could fall for someone if I have sex with them."

Rebecca moves closer to me and puts her hand on my shoulder. "It's just sex, Jake. Don't take it as a proposal for marriage, okay?" She suddenly kisses me hard, her hands moving over the back of my head and around my neck as she pulls me to her. I can feel her soft, round breasts pressing against me as we allow our passions to flow. I have to wonder if what's happening will upset Raina or Dominique.

She opens my pants and then pulls them to the floor to expose my rapidly growing cock. Rebecca then goes down, opening her mouth and allowing my cock to slide into her mouth. I buck a little as she allows the end of it to drive into the back of her throat. The sensation is amazing as Dom's wife gently sucks on it.

"Oh, shit," I moan as she massages my balls with her hands. "You're good at this," I whisper as she gags on my rod a couple of times. Looking over at where Raina is with Mike, I can see that they have already noticed what's happening here. They are discussing the fact that Rebecca is giving me head and that turns me on.

Dara has already begun to suck on Dom's hard cock as he sits back in his seat. I figured it would only be a matter of time before she decided she wanted him. A lot of the sexual tension between all of us was coming from her, anyway. Dara is a very sexual woman, though she probably prefers to save herself mostly for her husband, Mike.

Rebecca sucks on my cock for a while before she takes off her clothes and then straddles me. She slowly lowers her soft, wet pussy down onto me and begins to ride me. I can feel her cervix each time she drops down, and I wonder how long I will be able to withstand her sexual energy before I come inside her. The others notice what is going on and turn to watch as Rebecca's soft body rocks on top of me.

"Oh, Jake," she moans as her fingers massage her little nub at the top of her labia. "Oh, baby. Come inside me, okay? Come hard for Becca."

"Fuck," I mutter as I reach up and feel her soft breasts in my hands. Though her mammaries are larger than Raina's, her dark pink nipples are smaller. Gently running a finger over each one, I watch as my lover's body reacts to the stimulation. She loves that I'm playing with her this way, and so do I.

"Your cock feels so good inside my pussy," she tells me. "I've wanted you inside me since last night, Jake. Oh, baby. You're made for my pussy."

The others continue watching as we fuck hard for several minutes. My balls begin to ache with anticipation as I get closer and closer to coming with her. Rebecca's pelvis grinds into me as we work closer to our mutual climaxes. She loves my cock inside her, and I am thoroughly enjoying feeling her on top of me.

"Oh, fuck," I say as I suddenly begin to come. *"FFFUUUUCCCCKKKK..."* I spurt hard inside my lover's tight pussy, her wet lips gripping the sides of my cock as she continues to move up and down on me. *"Ohhhhh...OHHHHH!!!"* My toes curl as I feel every inch of her sweet cave. Dominique is a lucky man to have a woman as sexual as his wife. That's not to say that I am not happy with Raina, but right now Rebecca is getting more jism out of my balls than I have lost in a long time.

*"Uhhh...UHHHH!!!"* Rebecca's body moves wildly on top of me as she orgams. *"Baby...baby...oh, Jake...baby...ohhhhh..."* Her wet juices slowly move down onto me as her body gives in completely to her orgasm. *"Ohhh...baby..."*

We grind into each other until we finish and then Rebecca rolls off me. Sitting back on the sofa, I look at the others who have watched us together. They appear to now have the same idea as they turn and begin to enjoy each other in the same way. Raina's legs are soon back so that Mike can enjoy the taste of my wife. My own mouth waters as I watch them, but I soon have my attention taken by the woman beside me as she cleans off my cock with her mouth. Rebecca loves making love and doing everything that surrounds that process.

"Oh..." I turn to see Dominique's large cock buried deep inside Mike's wife. Dara's face is red as he fucks her hard. *"Ohhhh..."* Her toes are pointing as she begins a long, gentle orgasm with the other man. Her eyes wide, Dara squirts a little, her juices coating Dom's stomach as she does. He doesn't take notice as he empties his balls into her, though. I wonder if he is thinking at all about Mike and how in some way he is getting back at him by fucking his wife.

Raina and her lover are fucking doggy style as she is on her hands and knees. Mike pulls at my wife's ass as his cock moves in and out of her. They are both in the throes of passion together as they orgasm, their bodies colliding as he fucks her hard. Raina grinds her ass into the other man as he fills her with his salty man gravy. Seeing this makes me hard again, and Rebecca takes advantage of this as she reaches out and grips my pole.

"You like seeing her having sex, don't you?" she giggles.

"Yeah, I guess I do," I answer her. "It's just so different from what I have seen."

"It is, huh?" Rebecca giggles before pulling on my cock and moving her hand to my ball sack. "You had a lot for me, didn't you."

Smiling, I tell her, "You are a hot woman, Becca. I think we know that's why I got off so well."

She winks at me before getting up from the sofa and going to collect her clothes. The others as they finish do the same thing and we each find our own spouse. Raina takes my hand and leads me to the bedroom where we will be sleeping. Without saying a word, she takes me inside and begins to suck on my cock. It seems that something has been awakened in my wife and she wants to experience it with me after we have both made love with other spouses.

# Chapter Eight: Deeply Involved

My wife and I go to the game room in the cabin and sit down near the pool table. She seems taken with what happened last night between us and the other couples.

"That was very intense last night, Jake."

"Yeah, it was," I agree as I nod my head. "Rebecca was very much into what we were doing."

Raina shakes her head. "You both were really into it, weren't you?"

Smiling, I tell her, "We were. And I think that everyone else was, too. Even you and Mike were having fun."

My wife blushes. "Yes, I think Mike and I really enjoyed our time together. There was just something about connecting with him. It was so intimate. It was so deep."

I reach over and take her hand. "Honey, this was the sort of thing that I think we've always wanted to do. You and I have never had the chance to do this, but when we did it last night it was wonderful. Don't you agree?"

Raina nods her head. "I can't believe that I'm saying this, but yeah, it really was fun. The white Mike touched me and the way we kissed was just something completely different than what I thought it would be."

"Has it changed what you think about her own marriage?" I ask.

"Of course not," she replies. If anything, I think it might actually strengthen our marriage if we agree to continue doing this."

"So you're happy with what we did?" I watch as my wife's cheeks become a little pink. This is a reaction that I don't see in her very often. Honestly, I'm a little aroused while being around her as she looks at me and considers my question."

"I'm actually very happy, yes. But is it something we can continue to do? Is there a point where you and I may become jealous of each other?"

I chuckle. "Raina, we have been married long enough that we know we love each other too much for that. Our marriage is strong and we can do this. Remember, we're only going to be in the cabin for another day or so. It's not as if we're going to have to go home with any of these other people. What happens here will stay here, honey. That's the beauty of this whole thing, right?"

Rayna moves closer to me and she looks into my eyes. "I hate what those bank robbers did to us by putting us in this cabin. But maybe we should thank them. Were it not for the fact that we're in here together, we would have never come to the conclusion that we could do this with other people."

"Are you saying that you'd like to swing with other people, honey?" I smile as I look into her face.

"If this is really swinging, then yeah, I really like it."

Smiling, I put my hand on her lap. "You know, we could keep doing this when we get out of here. It doesn't have to end once we walk away. There are other people who like to do this sort of thing, Raina."

We sit quietly in the game room for a while as we think about what we've said. Perhaps we've come upon a different way of doing things that we could get used to. My wife and I have always been simply a couple. I'm beginning to think, though, that there's room for others in our marriage. Maybe if we got together with other people more often and explored these sorts of things, we would be even happier. That's what Raina is beginning to think as well.

"Let's go talk to the others, okay?" My wife gets up from where she's sitting and I also do the same. We make our way to the living room where the others in the house are sitting and talking. As we get there, there's a smile on Dara's face.

"So what were the two of you up to? Dara asks.

Raina laughs. "Wouldn't you like to know?" The others in the room laughed with us for a moment before we sit down and begin to talk to them. "Jake and I have come to some conclusions. We really liked what we did together last night with some of you and we were thinking that maybe we could do that again."

"Yeah, we've been talking a lot about that as well," Mike says. "Even Dominique seems to have gotten over the idea of his wife doing something with another guy."

"Shut up, asshole," Dom replies.

"Baby, don't be that way," Rebecca says to her husband. "You know it's true. You told me last night, after we went to bed, that you really loved seeing me with another man. You should just admit that you liked what happened and then we can go on from there."

Dom frowns as he looks at his wife for a moment. His eyes roll around a bit as he looks at the rest of us as well before he talks to us about what really has been bothering him. "None of you, except for my wife, knows that we have had problems with our marriage in the past. Some of the problems we've had is that we've had trust issues. There were reasons for that, and I think that Rebecca has gotten over the trust thing. The thing is, I'm still having some problems with that."

My wife decides to get involved with the conversation at this point. "What sort of trust issues have the two of you had in the past?" I watch as her therapist's mind begins to work on how to help them solve their problems.

Rebecca sighs. "It all goes back to a time when Dom and I were having some problems with the frequency of sex in our marriage. He wanted sex most of the time and I didn't want sex as much as he did. There was a friend of mine that lived next door to us at the time, and she would come over to the house once in a while. Dom began to take notice of her and it didn't take very long for the two of them to begin doing some things that I didn't agree with."

"What sort of things?" My wife asks.

The other woman blushes as she looks at her husband. "I came into our house one day late from work and went back to our bedroom and found Dom lying on the bed while this other woman was giving him a blowjob."

"Oh wow, big guy," Mike comments. "You were a busy guy when she wasn't around, weren't you?"

"Please, let's not snipe at him," my wife says. Raina then looks at the couple and asks, "Have the two of you sought counseling for this?"

"No, we haven't," Dom answers. Rebecca says that she's over it and that I'm forgiven and everything is okay, but I know that it's not. It can never be okay because what I did was I ruined her friendship with that woman. I did it in a way that broke the vows of our marriage and I'm ashamed of that." He looks at his wife for a moment before telling her, "I'm so sorry for what I did to you. I know it was wrong and I never ever want to do that to you again. That's why what's been happening here has been bothering me a little. Even seeing you with Jake has caused me to think that maybe you would prefer just to have someone else because of what I've done in the past."

"Oh baby, you know that's not true. You're the only one for me. I married you and I love you now as I did then. Look, the other girl, Cindy, wasn't a very good friend. She was always sneaky and she went behind my back to do all sorts of things and that included going after you. We're both better off now that she doesn't live by us anymore, and honestly, I would never let that woman back into my house. She seduced you, and you were weak enough to let her do it, but that's okay. It was only a blowjob and there's nothing more to it. It was not love. You didn't fall in love with her and you didn't go with her. You're still with me, so we're okay, baby. Honestly, Dom. We're okay."

The couple lean into each other and they passionately kiss for a little while. Raina smiles with tears in her eyes as she watches the two of them together. It's obvious that they still love each other deeply and they want to be with each other. What has happened here in the cabin over the last couple of days has caused all of us to reconsider what our marriages really are like. Yes, there can be sex in a marriage without love, but there can also be sex with other people outside of the marriage. The idea of swinging with other people really appeals to me and I think it appeals to most of the other people in the room. This is something I think that we're probably going to continue looking at as we spend our time here together.

"Fuck the bank robbers," Mike says. "Fuck them all straight to hell. They have no idea that they've actually done us all a favor by putting us here in this cabin. It's funny that they think they've gotten away with something when in fact they've actually allowed us to figure out some things about ourselves. I don't know about the rest of you, but I've really enjoyed being here with you."

Dom looks over at him and laughs. " Even with me, you asshole?" The two men laugh as they look at each other. Though they have grated on each other since being here, they seem to be getting along much better now. There continues to be some light ribbing between them, but they're working things out. After hearing about the problems that Dom and his wife have had in their marriage, it seems that Mike is becoming a little more understanding. Maybe this will allow the rest of our time together to be more enjoyable.

"So when do you think they'll send the police to let us out of this cabin?" Dara asks.

"I don't know," I reply. "They said in two or three days, and we're coming up on the third day, so possibly very soon."

She frowns. "I hope they take a little longer to get here. I think we could have a lot more fun if we had more time. This is new for all of us, but it's really been very good for all of us, right?"

Rebecca nods her head. "I know I've had a great time with you all. We would have never met each other had it not been for the bank robbery and the fact that they put us in this cabin together. Maybe once they get caught we should all thank them for that and chip in for their legal fees." We all laugh after she makes this comment. Of course, none of us are going to give any money to those guys, but we do owe them a little something for the way they've put us together. It's not the circumstances any of us would have chosen on our own, but we have made the best of it in many ways. We still have a little time to experiment a bit more and I know we're going to do that. It's going to be interesting to see just what happens next.

# Chapter Nine: Keeping Things Clean

I'm standing in the bathroom when I hear somebody walk in behind me. "Hey there, Jake. What are you up to?"

I turn around to see Dara standing behind me. "Oh, hey, Dara. I'm just getting ready to shave." I notice that she's wearing only a bra and a pair of panties.

She grins wickedly at me. "Do you mind if I use your shower? The one in our bathroom isn't very hot."

"Sure, I guess so," I reply as I look at her. "I think the water in this shower is actually very hot."

"I'll bet it is," she says to me as she begins to take her clothes off. Dara then steps into the shower and turns the water on. I continue shaving as I look over at her once in a while through the clear glass windows of the shower doors.

For the next few minutes, Dara continues to shower. She takes her time shaving her legs and washing her hair, and I can't help but continue to watch her. I notice that I'm beginning to become just a little aroused as I watch her. Raina isn't around at the moment to keep an eye on what I'm doing, so after I finish shaving I just sit and watch the other woman through the door.

"You're a naughty boy," she says with a giggle as she notices. "Do you like to watch me, Jake?"

I feel goosebumps rise along the back of my neck. "I'll admit that I don't mind seeing you right now." We both laugh at my answer.

"Have you had a shower this morning yet?"

Shaking my head, I tell her, "No, I haven't yet. I was going to do that in a little while."

She opens the shower door. "There's plenty of room in here, don't you think? I could use a little help getting clean, anyway." Dara smiles as she winks at me. It doesn't take any more coaxing to convince me to take off my clothes and step into the shower with her. After the door closes, her hands move to my body as Mike's wife puts soap all over me.

"Oh," I say as she moves to my manhood. "Yeah, I guess that could be dirty, huh?"

"We have to keep everything clean, sweetie. You were taught that as a kid, right?" She looks into my eyes as she rubs my cock slowly. There is no doubt where this is going as the beautiful woman in the shower with me works to bring me to climax.

"Here," I say as I take the soap from the shelf in the shower. I put some on my hands and rub it all over her back and then her arms and sides. Dara takes one of my hands and pushes it to her soft labia.

"Don't miss this part," she tells me. "Get the little hairs about my clit, too."

My fingers slip around her lovely muff for a while as she directs me where to go. Dara begins to grind into my hand as I pleasure her little lady bud, and the end of my cock presses into her back. The two of us begin to enjoy our shower together as we get closer to coming.

"Fuck me," she says to me quietly before turning and kissing me hard. Dara's full lips are sweet as they press against mine. Our tongues move into each other's mouths as we search for the passion between us. We have been with other people in this cabin so far, and it's time that we enjoy each other together.

I turn her back around and pull her hands up to put them on the wall of the shower. "You're a fucking whore," I growl as I begin to want her more than I wanted Rebecca yesterday. "Dammit, I want you."

She giggles as she spreads her legs. I press my cock against her wet opening and easily slide into her. Dara's body jerks a little as I seat the head of my manhood against her firm cervix. It's not very deep and I look forward to pounding it hard with my cock.

"Oh, fuck," she moans as I pull her ass toward me. "Oh, Jake. Fuck. You're deep." Her hands move along the wall of the shower as she attempts to hold on. "Damn, you're so deep, sweetie. Fuck."

We move together as we quietly fuck under the water from the shower's head. I hear my wife walk into the bathroom while talking to someone. She soon sees what we are up to in the shower and she smiles.

"You two decided to do something without us, huh?" Dominique is standing just to her side.

"That looks like fun," he adds with a grin. The two of them begin to take off their clothes and they step into the shower after doing so. Dom reaches for Raina and kisses her hard as he fingers her soft, hairless pussy. She wriggles around in his arms as he sinks his fingers into her, finding my wife's G-spot easily.

"Do it like that," she tells him as her labia hug his fingers tightly. "That's nice, Dom. Do that." She reaches for his swollen pole and rubs it with her hand. He groans as she does this and some precome trickles from the end of it. Raina smears it all over him as he lifts her up and pushes her back against the shower wall. I watch as he sinks his cock into her and they begin to fuck.

"You're so damned tight," he tells her as his balls strike her ass. My wife's legs are wrapped tightly around him as she enjoys his cock inside her. "You're so fucking tight."

"I'm his whore," Dara tells the others. "I'm Jake's fucking whore." She grinds into me as I thrust even faster. I am very close to losing my load inside Mike's wife as I pull her hard to me. All I want at this moment is to leave all my spunk deep inside her. Maybe she'll get pregnant? It doesn't matter to me as I enjoy fucking her regardless. Whether Dara is on the pill or not is of no consequence to me.

"Shit, I'm close," I tell her. "Dammit."

"Wait on me," she pleads. "Don't come without me, Jake. I want to feel you getting off inside me when I finally come, okay? Wait for me."

I don't know if I can honor her request. Her soft, tight pussy feels more amazing than Rebecca's. It could be the way we are having sex right now that makes everything feel so much more intense. Biting my lip, I try to keep my mind on just pleasing Dara as I thrust in and out of her sweet snapper. Reaching forward, I play with her small, pink nipples, which seems to help her move along.

"Holy fuck, Jake. Holy...*ahhhhhh*..." Dara squirts a little as she orgasms. *"OHHHH!!! COME WITH ME!!! OHHHHH!!!"*

*"Fuck! Uhhhh..."* I spurt hard into my lover as we grind into each other. My balls force my liquid love deep into Dara's sweet quiff as I pull on her nipples. *"Gahhhh...OHHHHH!!! FUCK!!!"* The intensity of the orgasm for me is much greater than any I have had before as I empty into Mike's wife. Her pussy is tight and it feels amazing to spurt what I have into her.

"Oh...*ohhhhh*..." My wife comes just as I pull out of Dara, Dom's large cock moving quickly in and out of her wet hole. *"UHHHH...OOOOHHHHH!!! DOMMMM!!!"* Raina's fingers run through her lover's hair as he fills her pussy with his love sauce. Though he comes, he doesn't say much as his balls slap hard against my wife. The aroma of sex is thick in the wet shower, and after they finish what they are doing we all wash ourselves off and get out.

We go into the bedroom and find Mike going down on Rebecca in our bed. His tongue is moving through her soft folds as she is coming.

"Ohh, baby. *Ohhhhh...uhhhhh*..." Her eyes are closed as she enjoys his tongue flicking along her lady bud. *"Mmmmm...fuck...ohhhhhhh..."*

Mike doesn't wait for her to finish before pushing her legs back and pushing his cock into her. He humps her fast and hard as her husband stands a couple of feet away and watches. There is nothing said between any of us as we become an audience for the both of them.

"I'm fucking your wife," he chuckles as he looks at Dom. "She's fucking nice, man. I'm going to come inside her." He laughs as his long shaft goes deep into Rebecca's pussy.

"Do it," Dom says with a sly grin. "Give her everything you've got, Mike. Don't hold back, you asshole." The two men laugh as Mike breathes hard. Soon, he begins to orgasm as Rebecca wriggles around on the bed beneath him.

"*Yeesssss. YEEEESSSSS!!!*" He comes inside her as her legs are wrapped around him. "*Fuck! FUCK!!! OHHHH, FUCK!!!*" Mike soon finishes and pulls out of his lover before collapsing on the bed beside her. Rebecca, happy to have had another man on top of her, rolls over and puts his cock in her mouth in the same way she did for me after we had finished making love.

"This is AWESOME!" Dara smiles big as she looks at her husband on the bed. "You did it, sweetie! I told you it would be fun, right?" She jumps onto the bed and into her husband's arms.

"Damn, this has been a really crazy couple of days," Dom says with a laugh. "It will probably be over soon, though."

"Maybe so," I reply. "But at least we will have each other until it is actually over. The cops are bound to find us by tonight or tomorrow and then it will be back to our boring lives."

Raina looks at me and shakes her head. "I don't think I'm going back to the way things were before, baby. No, we should consider swinging even after getting out of here."

"Really?" She smiles and nods her head.

"You know, she has a point," Rebecca adds. "We could all get together after all this is over."

"We live in California, Becca," Dom points out. "It's not like we will be down the street from them."

"We could move," she suggests to her husband.

"Uh, no. I have work there and it pays well." He shakes his head while looking at the rest of us. "I'm sure we will come and visit some, though."

"You had better, man." Mike smiles as he looks up at Dominique. "It's not you I really want to see, though." He winks at Rebecca as she lies on the bed nearby.

"Maybe we can play spin the bottle again tonight? With a sex twist?" Dara suggests.

"Maybe we should do that," I agree. The six of us leave the bedroom and go to the living room to spend more time together. We leave our clothes behind as there really is no reason to keep them on at the moment. There will be more sex tonight unless the police arrive to free us from this cabin. I have no doubt about that.

# Chapter Ten: Freedom Comes Early

The next morning comes early for us. A little before five o'clock in the morning, the police arrive to free us. We are startled as the door is broken down, and several men in black clad uniforms march in.

"Is everyone alright?" one of the officers calls out to us.

"We're all safe," I yell back to them. I come running down the stairs with my wife close behind me. "Did you catch them? Did you catch the bank robbers who put us in this cabin?"

The lead police officer shakes his head as he looks at me. "You people are here because of some bank robbers?"

"Of course we are," Dom replies. "Didn't you people get a phone call to come get us out of here?"

Another of the officers steps forward. "We got a phone call about some odd things going on in this cabin and that there could be someone hurt. It's actually owned by one of the state senators here and he wanted us to check on it after he got a phone call from a friend of his who is a hunter. What's this about a bank robbery?"

"Damn, I say as I look at the officers. Three days ago we were in a bank and some robbers came in, took some cash and then took six of us with them. They said we were going to be hostages until they got out of the state. They promised they would call the authorities once they got out and you would come get us."

The police officers look each other and they began to talk about what it is we've told them. It appears the bank robbers never called anyone at all and instead just left us here. I walk over to the front door and I look outside, realizing there wasn't even a sheet of plywood outside the door. There are a couple of sticks that have been screwed to the door, probably to make it sound to us like they were actually putting up a large sheet of plywood. It looks like the whole time that we were here, we were here without actually being hostages.

"Shit," I say as I laugh. "They pulled one over on us. Can you believe this?" I motion for the others to come take a look at the door, and as they do, they begin to laugh.

"But they kidnapped us," Dara says. "We were taken against our will and they dropped us off here. Are you saying that they put us in some state senator's cabin?"

The lead police officer simply nodded his head and replied. "Yeah, that's what it looks like. We had gotten a report of hostages taken and we had been keeping our eyes out for any signs of you. But it seems that the robbers are long gone."

"What now?" I ask.

"All of you will have to go back with us to the station. We'll have to debrief you and talk about what actually happened here as well as get a description of the robbers if you're able to give one."

"I see." I look at the others with me and we all begin to shake hands and embrace. "Well, it looks like after all we've been through, this was all just a giant joke to the robbers. I'll bet they were laughing the whole way as they left the state."

"That's if they left the state," my wife points out. "They could still be in the area, we don't know. They lied to us about this being a place for us to stay until they called the police, right? So they could be anywhere. They could be in Denver."

We all gather our things and go with the police officers back to their station. As we are sitting there together, we go through all the things we know about the robbers as well as the vehicle they were driving. The officers take lots of notes and they ask us lots of questions to go along with them. We continue to relive the whole thing all over again, minus the sex we enjoyed together. There really is no reason to tell them about that. Even though we know soon we're going to have to go our separate ways, we put on brave faces and do what we can to ensure the criminals are found and prosecuted to the fullest extent of the law.

A few days later, my wife and I go back to the same bank. Once again we meet the manager and we talk to him about the account. We also talk about what happened with the bank robbery. He assures us this will not happen again, but we're not so certain. Raina and I have additional concerns that he's unable to help us resolve, so we soon leave and we make our way down the street towards a small restaurant. As we go inside, the smell of fresh cooked food fills our nostrils.

"I hear they have great apple pie here," Rayna says. Maybe we can get some for here and then take some back home. Wouldn't you love little apple pie, sweetheart?"

Smile at her and nod my head. "Sure, I think apple pie would be great. Maybe even a hamburger. I'm really hungry for a hamburger after spending all that time in the cabin and having to eat canned foods."

"It wasn't so bad, though, was it?" She asks.

"Not really. We got to meet some really interesting people and then we got to do some things we never thought we would do. It was a great time if you forget about the fact we were forced to be there in the first place."

My wife and I eat our pie, and as we do, there's another couple that sees us. They smile and we smile back at them, though we don't know who they are, and soon they come to sit down at our table. They too have some apple pie and they just want to talk.

"Hey, my name is Greg and this is my wife, Sara." They both reach over to us and we shake their hands. "So, we just moved into the community and we're wondering if there's anything fun to do on the weekends around here."

My wife nods her head as she looks back at them. "There are lots of great things to do around here. If you like the city life, there's some nice nightclubs and other places that you can visit. But if your thing is the great outdoors, of course we've got the Rocky Mountains and all the other places surrounding us. It's a great place to live if you can get used to the winters being so cold."

Sara nods her head and smiles as she looks back at us. "We're from Alaska, so we're actually very used to the cold weather. I think we'll actually have a pretty easy time of it during the winters here in Colorado."

"Alaska, huh?" I say as I smile. What part of Alaska did you live in?"

"Juneau," Greg tells me. "It's not such a terrible place to live, as long as you can get over the fact that everything is so expensive and it's hard to get anywhere in the winter. Honestly, Colorado has been a huge upgrade so far."

"Welcome to Colorado, then," my wife says to them.

The four of us continue to have a very nice conversation while eating our pie. Eventually, though, Greg and Sarah began to talk about something that sounds very familiar. Raina and I are a little surprised that they would talk about this sort of thing in public at all.

"I know this is going to sound really weird, but are there any swingers clubs in Denver?" Sara asks.

I can feel my face turning red as I look at the two other people. Do they know about us? Have they heard something about us and they're trying to figure out whether it's true or not? I can't be certain as I continue to look at them. I eventually turn to look at my wife and can see that she's thinking along the same lines.

"I'm not sure about that," Raina says cautiously. "Are you both into that lifestyle?"

Greg looks over at his wife and he says to her, "You shouldn't have said anything to them. That's not something you talk about in mixed company, Sara."

"No, no, that's all right," I tell him. "As a matter of fact, we're sort of in that lifestyle as well."

"Seriously?" Greg raises his eyebrows as he looks at me and my wife. "You're not kidding around with us, are you?"

"Absolutely not. We're new to it, though, so we have no idea about any clubs or things of that nature."

"I see." Greg takes a breath before asking, "Are you both clean?"

"Clean?" Raina appears to take offense as she replies, "We are professional people, Greg. We don't go around hiring street hookers or anything like that. Neither of us have or ever will use drugs and we don't have diseases, if that's what you mean."

"I'm sorry. That was the wrong way to get this conversation going," he admits. "Sara and I are new to this as well. We've been with one other couple in Alaska and they told us we should look for a good club to join if we want to really get into swinging."

"Makes sense," I say while nodding my head. "But we have no clue about any of them."

"The internet probably can give you several names of clubs, I would guess," Raina says. "Don't start asking if people are clean if they look clean, okay? It makes them feel like you're judging them in some way."

"I apologize," Greg says while shaking his head. "It's just an important thing to know."

As I study the couple, I can see that they are a few years younger than us, but very similar in their personalities to us. I begin to think about what it would be like to put Sara's legs back and fuck her hard. She's beautiful, after all, her auburn hair pulled back into a sexy ponytail as she looks at us with her hazel eyes.

"I have an idea," I say to everyone at the table. "Why don't we get together for dinner tonight and just enjoy getting to know each other."

Sara smiles softly. "Do you mean that we would have sex, then?"

"I don't know. Maybe. It's important to get to know each other first, don't you agree?"

"I agree," she replies. "Is that what we would be doing, then? Getting to know each other and then having sex?"

Raina laughs. "Do you want to have sex with my husband?"

Sara studies me for a minute before she replies, "He would nut in less than two minutes with me."

"What?" I laugh nervously as I look at the young woman across the table. She appears very resolute in her ability to handle me easily as she grins at me.

"I'm sorry. Sara sometimes can be a little forthright."

"Greg says I'm a nympho. Do you think I might be a nympho, Jake?"

"Shit."

Raina smiles and allows a giggle to slip. "Wow. You're good at this, aren't you?"

The other woman smiles and laughs a little. "I like men. That's why we do what we do, right baby?"

"Right," Greg replies while shaking his head.

"So, you'll get me off in two minutes, huh?" I say to her with my own smile. "You're that good?"

Sara leans toward me and looks into my eyes. "Guaranteed."

"Oh, this is getting spicy now," Raina says while laughing. "You two would be a real pair in bed, huh?"

"Let's find out," I say as I get up from my seat. "I'll cover the pies, if that's okay with you two."

Greg's wife replies, "You'll cover my pie when I tell you to, Jake."

My cock is rock hard as I turn and go to the counter to pay for the food before the four of us leave to go straight to our house. I can't believe the luck we have just had in finding our next swinging partners. Raina and I will soon be enjoying the other couple in bed with us and Sara will get the chance to show me just how quickly she can make me nut. Though I'm skeptical that she can do it in under two minutes, I have an open mind to such things. I'll wait to pass judgment on her abilities until at least Tuesday. Or maybe even Wednesday."

THE END

Did you love *Swingers To Captive Lovers - A Wife Watching Multiple Partner Wife Sharing Romance Novel*? Then you should read *Hotwife Exchange For Debt Payments - A Hotwife Wife Sharing Wife Watching Romance Novel*[1] by Karly Violet!

[2]

**Would you willingly allow another man to take your wife to repay a debt of $100k?**

This was precisely the situation that Layden found himself in.

When out of thin air, he found $100k had suddenly appeared in the joint account he shared with his wife, Terri

The naive husband was confident the money belonged to him and pursued speculative investments that were doomed to fail

And when they did indeed fail, it transpired the money was transferred to him erroneously from unscrupulous characters.

---

1. https://books2read.com/u/me9opr

2. https://books2read.com/u/me9opr

And when it became clear, there was no way to repay the sudden debt they were demanding ……..

……..**Layden has no choice but to consider loaning his wife's body as payment for debt!**

*This scorching hot 20,000 word novel features a naive husband suddenly finding himself in debt to a dangerous man with no option other than to loan his wife's body for repayment.*

Read more at https://www.patreon.com/karlyviolet.

www.ingramcontent.com/pod-product-compliance
Ingram Content Group UK Ltd.
Pitfield, Milton Keynes, MK11 3LW, UK
UKHW041932131224
452403UK00001B/77